Perfectly Princess

Yellow Princess Gets a Pet

by Alyssa Crowne

illustrated by Charlotte Alder

Scholastic Inc.

New York Toronto London Auckland
Sydney Mexico City New Delhi Hong Kong

For my mom, Carole,

who taught me to love animals.

And for Goldie,

a great dog and a real hero.

ISBN 978-0-545-20852-9

12 11 10 9 8 7 6 5 4 3 2 1 10 11 12 13 14 15/0

Printed in Jiaxing, China 68
Designed by Kevin Callahan
First printing, December 2010

Contents

Chapter One

A Very Special Day

Abby Larsen opened the yellow box where she kept her markers. She picked out a canary yellow one. It was darker than the lemon yellow marker. It was yellower than the golden yellow marker. Perfect!

Then Abby walked to the princess calendar that hung on her bedroom wall. Each month showed a picture of a different princess. Now it was May, and Abby liked the May princess a lot. She had wavy hair, just like Abby. She was standing in a field

of yellow and white flowers. Yellow jewels sparkled in her crown. She was even petting the mane of a beautiful white unicorn.

Underneath the picture were boxes for each day of the month. The first eleven days of May had big yellow Xs over them. Abby looked at the next box: May 12. She smiled.

"Today is the day!" she said.

Abby wanted to make sure she got this X just right. She took off her glasses. She wiped the lenses with a tissue to make sure there were no smudges. Then she put her glasses back on. Very carefully, Abby drew an X over the box.

She was so excited that she couldn't help jumping up and down. She put the marker back in its box and then ran downstairs. Her mom and dad were in the kitchen.

"Mom! Dad! Today is the day!" Abby cried, running into the room.

MAY
12
TOYS

"You mean it's Saturday?" her dad asked. Mr. Larsen had a little smile on his face, like he was teasing.

"Not *just* Saturday," Abby replied. "Saturday, May twelfth."

"Yes, it is," said Mr. Larsen. "It is Saturday, May twelfth."

"Not *just* Saturday, May twelfth," Abby said. "Today we've lived in this house for exactly three months. And you know what that means!"

"It's time to clean the closets?" asked Mrs. Larsen. She was teasing, too. Abby could tell because she had one eyebrow raised.

But Abby was getting impatient. She twirled around on the kitchen floor.

"It's time to talk about getting a pet!" Abby cried. "You promised. You said after we lived here for three months we

could talk about it. And it's been three months exactly!"

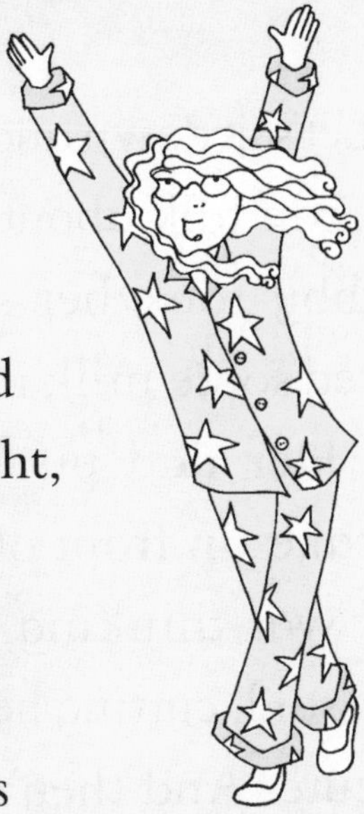

Mr. Larsen grinned and nodded. "Oh, right, a pet. How could I forget?"

Before they moved into the house, Abby's family lived in an apartment. There was a rule that you couldn't have pets there. That made Abby sad. She loved animals as much as she loved princesses. And the color yellow. And macaroni and cheese. She could have mac and cheese whenever she wanted. And she had lots of yellow princess things. But she couldn't have a pet . . . until today!

"Can we go get one right now?" Abby asked eagerly.

"Let's sit down and eat," Abby's mom said. "We can talk about it over breakfast."

Abby took her seat at the table. She poured some milk into her favorite yellow cup. Her dad put a plate of blueberry pancakes in front of her.

"I was thinking of getting a canary," Abby said, cutting her pancakes. "Canaries are cute. And they're yellow. But I'm not sure. You can't really pet them or cuddle with them."

"What about a dog?" asked Abby's mom. "I had a little brown dog when I was your age. You can pet a dog and play with it and everything."

Abby made a face. "Dogs are dirty and smelly and their hair gets everywhere. And they lick your face. Yuck!"

"Not all dogs are like that," said Abby's dad. "Plus, you can train them so they won't lick your face."

Abby shook her head. “No dogs,” she said firmly.

“What about a bunny?” asked Mrs. Larsen. “They’re cute and cuddly.”

Abby nodded. “I didn’t think of that! A bunny might be nice.”

Abby closed her eyes. She imagined herself in a field of yellow and white flowers, just like the May princess. A bunny hopped up to her. It was cute—but not as amazing as the unicorn in the picture.

“Hmm,” she said, opening her eyes again. “Maybe. But I’ve never seen a princess with a bunny rabbit before. I might need a pet that’s better for a princess. Like . . . a unicorn!”

“A unicorn would be a great pet for a princess,” agreed her mother. “It’s too bad they’re not real.”

“Then what about a pony?” Abby asked, feeling excited. “That’s almost like a unicorn, just without the horn."

"It's not easy to take care of a pony," her mom replied. "Besides, you need to live out in the country to have space for a pet like that."

"I know. A kitten!" said her dad suddenly. "They're cute and cuddly. And a princess would look great petting a kitten. Besides, I had a cat when I was a kid. It was a good pet."

Abby imagined herself as a princess once again. A tiny white kitten sat in her lap. She smiled.

"A kitten might be nice," she said. Then she sighed. "But kittens can be messy, too, can't they?"

Mr. Larsen laughed and looked at Abby's mom. "How did two messy people like us raise the neatest girl in the world?"

"It's good that Abby is neat," said Mrs. Larsen, grinning. She turned to her

daughter. "Abby, choosing a pet is a big decision. I don't think we should get a pet today. You should probably think some more, until you're sure about what you want. Then we can get the house ready for the new pet."

Abby was a little sad, but she knew her mom was right. "Okay," she said. "When I decide, I want to be totally sure!"

Chapter Two

The Perfect Pet for a Princess

Abby liked living in the new house. Her new bedroom had pretty yellow walls. It made Abby think of sunshine and flowers every time she woke up.

When Abby first moved, she was sad about leaving her friends behind. But she was lucky. There were lots of nice kids on her new block! Two of the kids were even in her class at school: Jia and Spencer.

Jia had black hair that she always wore in braids. She was really good at roller skating and knew all the songs on the radio. But best of all, Jia loved princesses, just like Abby!

Spencer had messy brown hair. His clothes always had dirt or crumbs on them. Normally, Abby didn't like messy things. But she liked Spencer a lot.

When Abby and Jia played princesses, Spencer played with them. He pretended to be a dragon. Sometimes he pretended to attack them, and Abby and Jia defeated him. Other times, he was a friendly dragon who helped them find treasure.

The friends usually played together on Saturdays. But on this Saturday, Abby didn't go outside right away. She had to figure out which pet was the best to get! Her dad helped her. They went on the computer and read about different kinds of animals. Mr. Larsen showed Abby how to print out pictures.

Abby was putting the pictures in a neat pile when the doorbell rang.

"I'll get it!" Abby cried. She jumped up from her chair and ran to the back door.

Jia and Spencer were standing there.

"Did you get your pet yet?" Jia asked eagerly.

"Not yet," Abby replied. "I still have to decide."

Spencer frowned. "Rats! I wanted to play with your new pet."

Abby shuddered. "Yuck! Please don't say the word 'rats.' Rats are so gross!"

Jia and Spencer followed her inside.

"My cousin Eddie has a pet rat," Spencer said. "It's white. It likes to eat apples out of his hand. I don't think it's gross."

"Well, a rat is definitely *not* on my pet list," Abby said.

Abby and her friends gathered around the kitchen table. She picked up the first picture in her pile. It showed an orange fish swimming in a bowl.

"Possible pet number one: a goldfish," Abby said.

"It's pretty," Jia said, "but you can't really play with it."

"You could take it to the movies," Spencer suggested.

"What do you mean?" asked Abby, giggling. "You can't take a fish to the movies!"

"Why not?" Spencer said. He grinned. "You could bring its bowl and put it on your lap."

"That's silly," Jia said. "Where would she put her popcorn?"

Spencer nodded. "Good point."

Abby turned over the next picture. It showed a bright yellow canary.

"Ooh, it's your favorite color!" said Jia.

"I know," Abby said. "I think a canary might be a nice pet."

"But you can't really play with a canary, either," Spencer said.

"Sure she could," Jia said. "She could teach it tricks."

"Like rolling over and fetching?" Spencer asked.

"Of course not! *Bird* tricks," Jia said. "Like . . . I don't know. Stuff that birds do."

"There's more," Abby said. She showed them a picture of a little white bunny with pink eyes.

Jia smiled. "Aw. He's so cute!"

"I know," Abby said. "But this one's even cuter." She held up a picture of a tiny white kitten playing with a ball of yarn.

"Awwwwwwwww!" Jia and Spencer said together.

"I think it's a good pet for a princess, don't you?" Abby asked.

Jia nodded. "It's the perfect pet for a princess."

"No, a *dragon* is the perfect pet for a princess," said Spencer.

"And so is a cat," Jia said, rolling her eyes.

"Well, I can't have a dragon for a pet," Abby said matter-of-factly. "But I can get a cat. My mom and dad said so."

Spencer flipped through the pictures again. "Hey, there's no dog in here," he said.

"That's because I don't want a dog," Abby told him.

"But dogs are the best!" Spencer said.

"They are," Jia agreed. "You can play catch with them and run with them and everything. I wish I had a dog."

Abby wrinkled her nose. "They're messy! And they drool all over you!"

Jia took the pictures from Spencer. She plucked out the picture of the kitten.

"You should get a cat," Jia insisted. "It's the best one."

Abby looked at the picture. The kitten was so cute! For the first time, she felt sure of what she wanted.

Abby's mom came into the room. "Would anybody like some juice or a snack?" she asked.

Abby ran up to her. "Mom! I know what pet I want—a kitten!"

"Are you sure?" Mrs. Larsen asked her.

Abby nodded. "Positive."

Abby's mom glanced at the clock. "Tell you what," she said. "One night this week, we'll go out and buy all the things a kitten needs. Then your dad can take you to the animal shelter next Saturday to pick out a kitten."

"I have to wait a whole week?" Abby asked, pouting.

"We have to make sure we do everything right," Mrs. Larsen told her. "The week will go by fast. You'll see."

"Okay," Abby said. She nodded at Jia and Spencer. "Come on, let's go. We have to get my room ready for my new kitten!"

Chapter Three

Lily

Every day that week, Abby put an X on her calendar. Saturday was getting closer and closer!

One night, she and her mom went to the pet store. They bought a litter box and a bed for the new cat. They also got kitten food and bowls for food and water. They found toys and even a playhouse covered in carpet. It looked just like a castle!

"This is a lot of stuff for one little

kitten!" Abby exclaimed, as they carried the bags to the car.

"Pets need lots of things," said Mrs. Larsen. "After you pick out your kitten, we'll take it to the vet. We'll make sure it's healthy and has all the shots it needs."

"Will it hurt?" Abby asked, squeezing her eyes shut.

"Only a little," said her mom. "Kind of like when the doctor gives you a shot. The kitten will be fine."

Finally, Saturday came. Abby woke up so early that she could still see the moon in the sky through her window. She ran into her parents' room, anyway.

"Dad! Can we go to the animal shelter now?" Abby asked.

Mr. Larsen sat up. His eyes were still closed. "Abby, it's too early. Go back to sleep."

Abby went back to her room. But she

couldn't fall asleep. She was too excited! She stared at the May princess instead.

"Soon I'll have a pet, like you!" Abby whispered. "It won't be a unicorn, but it will be just as good."

Finally, Abby drifted off to sleep again. When she woke up, her dad was awake and dressed.

"Let's get moving, sleepyhead," he said. "We have a kitten to adopt."

Abby moved as quickly as she could. She brushed her teeth, washed her face, and combed her wavy hair so it wouldn't look messy. She put on jeans and a white shirt with yellow flowers on it. Then she pulled on her white socks and yellow sneakers.

Abby ran downstairs. Her dad had put two bowls of cereal out on the table.

"Mom had to work at the bookstore today," he said. "She said we should

send her a picture of the kitten from my phone."

Abby ate as fast as she could. She made sure not to spill any milk on her shirt. Then she and her dad got into the car. There was a plastic cat carrier on the seat next to Abby. A wire gate blocked one end. Abby's new kitten would ride home in the carrier. A soft blanket on the bottom would keep the kitten warm and safe.

Luckily, it didn't take too long to get to the animal shelter. Abby couldn't wait! Mr. Larsen pulled into a parking lot in front of a white building. The sign on the door said TWIN OAKS ANIMAL SHELTER. A family with two kids was outside, walking a tiny dog on a leash.

Abby and her dad headed through the front door into the lobby. Abby's dad had to walk fast to keep up! A woman with a ponytail sat behind the lobby desk. On the wall behind the desk were two sets of swinging metal doors. Abby could hear lots of dogs barking behind them. She marched right up to the desk.

"Hi, I'm Valerie. Can I help you?" the woman asked with a smile.

"We'd like to adopt a kitten," Abby said, grinning widely. "A white one, if you have it."

"We have quite a few kittens that need good homes," Valerie said. "I can show them to you in a minute. First, I need to ask you some questions." She took a form out of a pile on her desk. "Do you have any other pets?"

"No," Abby's dad replied.

Valerie nodded and put a check on the form. "Have you ever taken care of a cat before?"

"I had one when I was a kid," said Mr. Larsen.

"And he's been teaching me," Abby added. "I'm going to take good care of it, I promise!"

Valerie smiled again. "I'm sure you will."

Valerie asked a few more questions. Then she stood up. "Let's go to the cat room," she said.

They were about to follow her when the doors behind her swung open. A big dog with shaggy yellow fur came bounding into the lobby. He ran right up to Abby's dad and put his paws on Mr. Larsen's chest! Abby's dad just laughed. "Down, boy!"

Then a man came running through

the doors next. "Rex! Sit!" he yelled. The dog backed off of Mr. Larsen and sat down.

"I'm so sorry," the man said, grabbing the dog's collar. "I was about to take Rex for a walk, but he got away before I could put on his leash."

"Are you adopting him?" Abby asked, staying a few steps away from the big dog.

"No, I just work here," the man said. "But I wish I could. He's a great dog."

"He sure is," said Abby's dad. He was kneeling down and scratching Rex behind the ears.

"Do you still want to look at the cats?" Valerie asked.

"Yes!" Abby cried. She tugged on her dad's sleeve. "Come on, Dad. It's time to find my kitten."

They said good-bye to Rex and followed

Valerie into the cat room. It was a bright, sunny room filled with big cages. Each cage held a grown-up cat. In the middle of the floor, colorful gates were set up to form a play area. Abby eagerly walked up to it.

Six kittens were playing inside the pen. Two were gray with white stripes. Two were orange. One was a mix of black and brown and white.

And the last one had all white fur!

Abby couldn't believe it. She knelt down to get a closer look. The little white kitten had pretty blue eyes.

"She's perfect," Abby whispered.

"Would you like to hold her?" Valerie asked.

Abby nodded, and Valerie picked up the kitten and put her in Abby's lap. The kitten curled up right away. She looked up at Abby with her blue eyes. Abby

gently stroked the fur on top of her head. The kitten twitched her nose and purred happily.

"Dad, can we get her?" Abby asked.

"I think so," her dad said. "As long as Valerie says it's okay."

Valerie nodded. "I think you'll give the cat a good home. She's yours. Now you just need to name her."

Abby looked down at the cat. She had always planned to name her pet after a flower. Flower names were so pretty!

"Dad, what's the name of that white flower we get at Easter time?" she asked.

"You mean a lily?" Mr. Larsen said.

"Lily," Abby repeated slowly. "That's perfect!"

Abby looked down at her new pet. "Come on, Lily. I want you to see your new home!"

Chapter Four

A Suspicious Sneeze

"So this is Lily," said Abby's mom, appearing in the doorway of Abby's room that afternoon.

Abby was playing with Lily in her kitty castle. Lily kept poking her head out of a hole in the top tower. Abby still couldn't believe how cute she was!

"Pick her up, Mom," Abby said. "She likes it."

"I've never held a cat before," said Mrs. Larsen. "Babies, yes, but no kittens."

Abby's mom reached down and gingerly picked up Lily. The kitten squirmed a little. Mrs. Larsen held Lily up to her face.

"She's adorable," said Abby's mom. "In fact, she's—*ACHOO!*"

Mrs. Larsen sneezed, and Lily nearly jumped out of her arms. She quickly put down the kitten.

"Sorry," she said. "That was—*ACHOO!*"

"Do you have a cold?" Abby asked.

"I don't think so," her mom replied. She sounded a little worried.

Then Jia and Spencer ran into the room.

"Your dad said we could come up," Jia said. "We can't wait to meet your kitten!"

"Hi, Jia. Hi, Spencer," said Abby's mom. "I'm going to go downstairs for a bit."

Mrs. Larsen left, and Jia and Spencer

got down on the rug and looked inside the kitty castle.

"I don't see her," Jia said.

"Me, either," Spencer added.

Abby looked through the castle window. "She must be hiding somewhere."

Then Jia started to giggle. "Look!" she cried, pointing next to Abby's bed.

Abby had a yellow princess hat shaped like a big cone. The hat was slowly moving across the rug—by itself!

Abby ran to the hat and picked it up. Lily was underneath! She looked up at Abby and then quickly scampered back into the castle.

"I think she wants to be a princess, too," Abby said, laughing.

"She's so cute!" Jia said.

"Not bad for a cat," said Spencer. "What did you name her?"

"Lily," Abby replied.

Spencer frowned. "I would have called her Snowball, I think."

"Well, her name is Lily," Abby said. She reached inside the castle and scooped up the kitten. "Want to pet her?"

Jia and Spencer eagerly gathered around Abby. They softly stroked the kitten's fur.

"We should play princess," Jia suggested. "Lily is our magical cat. Then a mean dragon kidnaps her, and we have to rescue her."

Abby hugged Lily to her chest. "But what if the dragon hurts her?"

"I won't, I promise," Spencer said. "I'll only pretend to be mean. I like Snowball."

"Her name is Lily!" Abby reminded him.

The three friends played with the kitten all afternoon. Then Abby's dad helped them take pictures of Lily so Abby could bring them to school the next day.

That night, Abby watched Lily eat her kitten food. Lily took tiny bites. Then she neatly licked her lips clean. At bedtime, Abby tucked Lily into her soft cat bed. She put it on the floor next to her own bed. As she drifted off to sleep, Abby watched her kitten curl up with a stuffed mouse toy.

Lily really was the perfect pet!

The next day at school, Abby couldn't wait to show everyone the pictures of her new pet. All of the kids in Miss Krupka's class wanted to see them.

"She's so cute!" squealed Lauren, who had glasses just like Abby's.

230
63
1

"I have three cats," said Ryan, a boy with red hair and freckles.

"I already got to hold Lily and pet her and everything!" Spencer bragged.

"Me, too!" said Jia proudly.

Miss Krupka clapped her hands. "Time to quiet down, class. Abby, congratulations on your new pet. I have a good book about cats you can read during reading time, if you want."

"Thanks, Miss Krupka," Abby said, beaming.

Abby felt so happy. When she first came to the new school, she didn't know anybody. But today she felt like the most popular girl in the class!

When the bell rang at the end of the day, Abby's mom was waiting outside, as usual. She always walked Abby home. Today she had a sad look on her face, but she tried to smile when she saw Abby.

"Hey, sweetie. How was your day?" Mrs. Larsen asked.

"Good," Abby replied. "How's Lily?"

"Abby, we need to talk about Lily," said her mom as they walked. "I was sneezing all night. I was sneezing all morning, too. So I went to the doctor. He gave me a test to see if I had allergies."

"What are allergies?" Abby asked.

"It's when your body gets sick from normal things, like flowers or pets," her mom replied. "When you're allergic to something, you might sneeze or wheeze."

Abby was starting to get a bad feeling. "What did the doctor say?"

Mrs. Larsen stopped. She kneeled down and put her hands on Abby's shoulders.

"He says I'm allergic to cats," she said softly. "Abby, I'm so sorry. I didn't know. I've never been around cats before."

Abby's eyes started to fill with

tears. "Can't you take medicine or something?"

Mrs. Larsen shook her head. "The allergy makes it hard for me to breathe. It could be dangerous. I'm so sorry, but we have to find Lily a new home."

Abby did not want to hear any more.

"It's not fair!" she cried, running down the sidewalk.

Chapter Five

Bad News

Abby didn't mean to run away from her mom. But she was so upset she didn't know what to do! When she got to Spencer's house, she turned and ran up to the porch.

Spencer was out on the porch, reading a book. "Abby, what's the matter?"

Abby started to cry again. She didn't know what to say.

Just then, her mom caught up. "I just told Abby some bad news," said Mrs. Larsen. "I have an allergy to Lily. I don't think we can keep her."

Spencer's mom stepped outside. She was a short woman with lots of wild, curly brown hair. Abby had always thought that Mrs. Burton was nice.

"Are you talking about the kitten Abby got yesterday?" Mrs. Burton asked. "Spencer told me she was very sweet."

"She's the sweetest kitten in the world," Abby said through her tears. "I don't want to give her away. I can't!" Abby hugged her mom's legs. She felt awful!

"Hmm," said Mrs. Burton. She paused for a minute. "I've always wanted a cat. I'll have to talk to Spencer's dad, but maybe we could adopt her."

Spencer's eyes lit up. "Then you could visit her whenever you wanted!" he added.

"That's awfully nice of

you," said Abby's mom, squeezing Abby's shoulders. "It might work, but I think we have to check with the animal shelter first."

"Let's go inside and make some phone calls," Spencer's mom said. She nodded to Spencer and Abby. "Anyone feel like some oatmeal cookies and milk?"

"Yay!" cheered Spencer.

Abby wiped her tearstained cheeks with her sleeve. "O-okay," she replied.

Abby and Spencer ate cookies and milk on the porch while their moms talked inside.

"I'll take good care of Snowball, I promise," Spencer said, patting her arm.

Abby felt like crying again. "You have to call her Lily! That's her name."

Spencer looked thoughtful. "How about Lily Snowball?"

"Maybe," Abby said. "That sounds

kind of nice." She sniffled. "I'm going to miss her so much!"

"You can come see her any time you want," Spencer said. "I mean it."

"Thanks," Abby replied. Spencer was being nice. And she didn't want her mom to be sick because of Lily. She didn't feel so mad anymore—but she still felt sad.

Just then, their moms came back outside.

"Good news," said Mrs. Burton. "I have to go to the shelter and fill out some papers. But it looks like we can keep Lily."

Abby's mom sat down next to her. "I know how badly you want a pet," she said. "So I had the doctor do a bunch of tests. The good news is that I am not allergic to birds or bunnies or dogs."

"No dogs!" Abby reminded her.

"We can go to the pet store tomorrow after school," Mrs. Larsen said. "They

have birds there we could look at. And they have a book with pictures of rabbits that need nice homes. Maybe you'll find a pet as good as Lily."

"No pet will ever be as good as Lily," Abby said sadly. "But maybe it would be okay to look."

Abby felt a little better after that. But that night, it made her sad not to see Lily asleep in her cat bed.

How will I ever find another pet as good as Lily? Abby wondered.

Chapter Six

A Big Surprise

The next day, Abby's mom took her to the pet store right after school. The store had rows and rows of pet food, pet toys, pet clothes, pet books, and anything else a pet could ever need. The store didn't sell big pets like cats or dogs. But they had lots of small pets.

First Abby and her mom walked past a big section of tanks filled with lizards, fish, and snakes.

"Ew!" Abby said, making a face.

"Are you sure you don't want a nice lizard?" Abby's mom asked with a smile. "We could make a little princess hat for it."

"Definitely not!" Abby exclaimed.

They walked some more and found a room with large glass walls. Inside, pretty small birds perched in cages. Two green parrots flew freely around the room.

Abby pressed her face against the glass. There were tiny brown finches, pretty bluebirds, and green cockatiels. One cage held three yellow canaries. Abby thought their yellow feathers looked like sunshine and lemonade at the same time.

A young man with curly dark hair walked up to them. He wore a red shirt that said PET PALACE on it.

"Would you like to buy a bird?" he asked.

"Yes," Abby replied, nodding firmly. "A canary."

The man smiled. "I'm Ben. Follow me. You can pick out the one you want."

Ben led Abby and her mom into the bird room. The two parrots were now resting quietly on a fake tree branch. Ben opened up the canary cage and held out his finger. One of the canaries hopped onto it.

"I've been taking care of them since they were babies," Ben told them. "They're all tame. But this is the nicest one."

"Will she get on my finger?" Abby asked.

"She might," Ben said. "Let's try."

Abby held out her finger. She was a little nervous. The canary was very pretty. But she couldn't imagine having a real live bird on her finger!

Ben held the canary up to Abby's hand. The little bird hopped right on.

"Hi there, little bird," Abby said in a high voice.

The canary sat for a minute, then flew back into her cage. She began to sing a pretty song.

Tweet tweet tweet tweet tweet!

"So, Abby, what do you think?" Mrs. Larsen asked.

Abby thought for a minute. A canary

couldn't cuddle up on her lap, like Lily did. But the canary was the most beautiful shade of yellow. She was friendly. And she sang such a nice song.

"I think I would like to have her as a pet," Abby said. "I'll name her Daisy."

Ben grinned. "That's a great name! I'll get a little box so you can take Daisy home. Then I'll help you get the things you'll need to take care of her."

It turned out they needed a lot of things to take care of Daisy. She needed a cage and a food bowl and a water bottle. She needed a swing to perch on. She needed a cover for her cage so she would be warm and quiet at night. And of course, she needed canary food.

Abby started to feel more and more excited on the ride home. She held Daisy's little box in her lap. She could feel the bird flapping around nervously inside.

"It's okay, Daisy," Abby told her. "We'll be home soon."

When they got home, Abby and her mom set up the cage in Abby's room.

"Daisy will probably get birdseed on your rug," Mrs. Larsen warned. "We'll have to vacuum a lot to keep things clean."

"I didn't think of that," Abby said, suddenly worried. She didn't like the idea of birdseed on her yellow rug.

But Daisy was so cute. Maybe a little birdseed wouldn't be so bad.

"It's okay," she said finally. "I'll vacuum every day. It's fun!"

Daisy was all settled in her cage when Mrs. Larsen's cell phone rang.

"That was your dad," she told Abby, when the call was done. "He said he has a big surprise for us."

"Maybe he has some bird treats for Daisy," Abby guessed.

A few minutes later, they heard the front door open. Abby and her mom ran downstairs.

"Dad, what's the surprise?" Abby asked.

But she didn't have to wonder for much longer. Because right then, a big, yellow dog ran through the open door. It jumped up on Abby . . . and licked her face!

Chapter Seven

Rex Ruins Everything!

"*Surprise!*" said Abby's dad.

Abby's mom put a hand over her mouth. "Oh my goodness," she said. "Jim, what did you do?"

"Please get him off me!" Abby yelped.

Her dad ran up and grabbed the dog's leash. "Sorry," he said. "Don't you remember this guy? It's Rex, from the animal shelter."

Of course Abby remembered. How could she forget a slobbery dog like Rex?

"What is he doing here?" Abby asked, wiping her face.

Mr. Larsen looked sheepish. "Well, I couldn't stop thinking about him. He just looked so sweet! And your mom isn't allergic to him. And he's yellow, your favorite color. . . ."

Abby's mom knelt down and started petting Rex's head. "He *is* very cute," she said.

"He is *not* cute!" Abby cried. "He's big, and his tongue is gross and sticky!"

"I know it's a big decision, and I shouldn't have made it without you two," her dad said. "But it just felt so right. And I'll take care of him. I'll walk and feed him and everything."

Abby had to smile a little bit. Her dad sounded like *her,* back when she was begging her parents to get a pet.

"So what do you say?" her dad asked.

"I think he's wonderful," said Mrs. Larsen. "It will be nice to have a dog in the house. But I also know that Abby doesn't like dogs." She turned to Abby. "You're not afraid of them, are you?"

"No," Abby said truthfully, eyeing Rex. He was drooling. "They're just too messy!"

"I'll clean up all of Rex's messes," her dad said. "And hey, did you know that the name Rex means 'king'? Every princess needs a king, right?"

Abby thought about that for a minute. She had to admit that Rex was cute. He had big, brown eyes and a soft, pink tongue. And his fur reminded her of that fairy tale where the straw got spun into gold. It was beautiful.

Besides, she could tell how much her dad wanted to keep Rex. She knew what that felt like.

"Okay," Abby said carefully. "Just make sure he stays out of my room."

"No problem," her dad said. He gave her a big smile and scratched Rex behind the ears.

Soon it was time for dinner. Rex was very interested in everything they were eating. He walked around the table, sniffing all of the plates.

"He's getting his nose all over my noodles!" Abby complained.

"Down, Rex!" Mr. Larsen said.

But Rex just kept on sniffing.

After dinner, Mrs. Larsen headed back to the pet store to get some things for Rex.

"I'll have to work extra hours on Saturday," she said. "We're spending all of our money on pets!"

Abby went straight up to her room. Everything was in order, just how she liked it. Daisy was happily singing on her perch. Abby's stuffed animals were lined up from smallest to biggest on top of her toy box.

Abby went to her dresser and picked out an outfit for school the next day. She did that every night, so she'd be ready in the morning. This time, she took out a yellow skirt with white polka dots. She chose a white shirt with ruffles on the collar to go with it. She carefully draped them over her desk chair so they wouldn't wrinkle.

Then Abby got a book from her shelf.

It was a collection of princess stories.

"How about a story, Daisy?" Abby asked. "I know. Let's do, 'The Princess and the Pea.'"

Abby read the story out loud to her new pet. Daisy chirped happily and swung on her swing as she listened. It made Abby smile. Daisy was a *much* better pet than a messy old dog!

Soon it was time for bed. Abby put the cover on Daisy's cage.

"Good night, Daisy," she said.

Her mom and dad both tucked her in that night.

"Be sure to close the door," Abby said. "I don't want Rex to get in."

"Don't worry," her dad said. "We'll close the door tight. Rex won't be able to get in."

But he was wrong.

When Abby woke up the next morning, she screamed.

Rex was in her room! He was asleep on her rug.

"Bad Rex," Abby said, jumping out of bed. "Come on, get out of here."

Then she noticed something. Rex wasn't just sleeping on her rug. He was sleeping on something else. Something white and yellow.

"My clothes!" Abby wailed.

Rex jumped up and happily wagged his tail. Abby picked up her clothes. They were covered in yellow dog hair. A brown paw print marked her white shirt.

Abby couldn't believe it. "Rex, you've ruined everything!"

Chapter Eight

Not Again!

Abby was in a grumpy mood all day at school. She didn't get to wear her polka-dot skirt. Instead, she wore a yellow and white striped shirt and white leggings. It was a good outfit. But it wasn't as good as the skirt.

At reading time, Abby finished the book Miss Krupka had given her. It was about a cat that gets lost in a big city. Abby got sad, thinking about Lily. If she hadn't had to give Lily away, they would never have gotten Rex!

At lunch, all Spencer could talk about was his new kitten.

"Yesterday we were playing with her mouse toy and she did a backward somersault!" he said proudly. "It was amazing."

"You should hear Daisy sing," Abby bragged. "She is the best bird singer in the whole world."

"Can we see her?" Jia asked. "We could come over after school."

Spencer shook his head. "Not me. We need to take Lily Snowball to the vet for her shots."

Abby turned to Jia. "You can come over. I just hope Rex doesn't ruin everything again."

"I can't believe your dad brought home a dog," Jia said.

"I saw him in your backyard," Spencer added. "He's a big dog."

"Big and messy," Abby said, with a frown.

"Can I pet him?" Jia asked.

Abby shrugged. "If you want. But he'll probably lick your face."

Jia made a face. "Gross!"

"Besides, Daisy is the best pet," Abby added.

"Lily Snowball is the best pet," Spencer said quickly.

Jia shook her head and held up her hands. "They're *all* the best! No fighting over pets!"

Abby and Spencer laughed.

After school, Mrs. Larsen walked Abby and Jia home.

"Did Rex get in my room while I was gone?" Abby asked.

"No, he didn't," her mom replied. "I

got a special gate so I can keep Rex in the kitchen when I go out."

"Good!" Abby said. She was happy to hear it.

"I can't wait to meet him," Jia said. "And Daisy, too."

When they walked through the front door of the Larsen house, Abby's mom stopped. "Uh-oh!"

Abby pushed past her. "What do you mean, 'uh-oh'?"

Then she saw it. The dog gate was down on the floor. Rex was not in the kitchen.

"My room!" Abby yelled. She dropped her backpack on the floor and raced upstairs. Jia ran behind her.

The door to Abby's room was open. Abby stepped inside and gasped.

Rex had taken every one of her stuffed animals off the toy box! He had piled them up in the middle of the rug. Now he was running in circles around them.

Jia giggled. "He is so cute!"

"This is not cute!" Abby protested. "It's a mess!"

"It's not so bad," Jia pointed out. "He didn't chew any of them up. And your bird is okay, too."

Daisy! Abby had almost forgotten about her. But Jia was right. Daisy was happily swinging in her cage.

Jia was on her knees, scratching Rex behind the ears.

"We should play princess," Jia said. "We could be two princesses lost in the mountains. And Rex can rescue us."

"I have a better idea," Abby said. "We can be two princesses. And we can send Rex to the dungeon!"

Jia frowned. "Why? What did he do?"

Abby put on her princess hat. She picked

up her princess wand and pointed it at Rex. "I hereby banish you to the dungeon!" she cried. "For the crimes of drooling, slobbering, and making a mess!"

Rex didn't seem to mind being banished. He happily wagged his tail.

Abby sighed. Why did her dad have to adopt such a messy pet?

Chapter Nine

A Bad Cold

The next morning, Abby woke up feeling bad. Her throat hurt. Her head hurt. Her nose felt stuffy.

When she went downstairs, her mom was dressed for work. Her dad sat at the table, drinking a cup of tea. He was wearing his robe and sniffling.

Mrs. Larsen took one look at Abby and knew what was wrong. "Oh, no, you're sick, too!" she said.

"Poor Abby," said her dad. "You have

a cold, just like me."

"ACHOO!" Abby sneezed. "Maybe it's an allergy. Maybe we're allergic to Rex."

Abby's mom felt her forehead. "You're warm. This is definitely a cold. Guess you and Dad will have to stay inside today." She turned to Mr. Larsen. "Should I stay home from work?"

Abby's dad shook his head. "We'll be all right. I'll take good care of Abby."

Rex walked up to Abby and looked at her with his big, brown eyes. It was like he knew something was wrong.

"Go away, Rex," Abby said crossly.

"Eat your breakfast," her mom urged. "Then I'll give you some cold medicine, okay?"

Abby nodded. She ate some oatmeal

and took the medicine her mom gave her. Then Mrs. Larsen kissed her good-bye.

"I know what we need," her dad said, standing up. "Lots of blankets and pillows. And lots of cartoons!"

Mr. Larsen set up blankets and pillows on the small couch for Abby. He set up the big couch for himself. Then he gave Abby the TV remote.

"Find something good for us to watch," he said.

Abby saw that it was time for *Princess Power* to come on. She flipped to the right channel and snuggled into the couch.

Rex trotted up to her. He looked at her again with his big, brown eyes. Then he put his paws up on the couch.

"No, Rex," Abby said. "You can't come up here."

Rex gave a little whine.

"No," Abby said firmly.

Rex walked around in a little circle. Then he lay down on the rug and peered at her. He looked so sad.

The look melted Abby's heart.

"Okay, you can come up," she said, sighing. "But no licking!"

Rex climbed up on the couch. He curled up around Abby's feet. He felt nice and warm and soft.

"So maybe you two will be friends after all," her dad said, smiling.

"Maybe," Abby said. "But he still can't come in my room."

"Let me know when you're hungry again," her dad told her. "I can make us some frozen pizza."

Abby yawned. "Okay, Dad."

Abby felt very comfortable and sleepy. She could feel Rex's belly move up and down as he breathed. It felt kind of nice. She slowly drifted off to sleep.

Woof woof woof!

Abby woke up with a start. Rex was barking very loudly. But he wasn't in the living room anymore. It sounded like he was barking in the kitchen.

Abby's dad woke up at the same time.

"Rex, what's the matter?" he asked. He sleepily climbed off of the couch and walked into the kitchen.

He quickly came running back out.

"Abby, get outside, now!" he said. "There's smoke in the kitchen!"

Chapter Ten

Rex Saves the Day

Abby ran to the front door. Rex ran right beside her. What was happening?

Her dad came out of the house a few seconds later, carrying Daisy's cage. At the same time, Mrs. Burton ran out of her house.

"I heard Rex barking, and when I looked out the window, I saw the smoke," said Mrs. Burton. "I called the fire department."

As soon as she finished her sentence,

Abby heard the loud whine of a fire engine. A big yellow truck turned down the corner of their block. Abby hugged her dad tightly.

Four firemen jumped off of the truck. They all looked very tall to Abby. They wore yellow coats, big black boots, and yellow helmets. Two of the firemen put on masks and ran inside the house. One of the other men walked up to her dad. He had a thick red mustache.

"What happened here?" he asked.

"I'm not sure," Mr. Larsen replied. "I got up to make lunch for me and Abby. Then I fell back to sleep. I woke up when I heard Rex barking." Then Abby's dad slapped his forehead. "Oh, no—the frozen pizza! I never took it out of the toaster oven!"

The fireman gave Rex a pat on the head. "I'm not sure why your smoke alarm

FIRE

didn't work. You're lucky you have this dog. He may have saved your lives."

The two firemen came back out of the house. One of them was carrying the toaster oven. It was all black and burned.

"Looks like we got one pizza here, extra crispy," the fireman joked. He opened the door of the toaster oven and Abby saw the burned pizza inside.

"What's it like in the house?" Abby's dad asked.

"A lot of smoke, but not much damage," the fireman replied. "We'll blow out the smoke with a big fan. You should be able to go back inside in a few hours."

"You can stay at our house until then," Mrs. Burton offered.

"Rex and Daisy, too?" Abby asked.

"Of course!" Mrs. Burton replied.

Everyone in the neighborhood came

to see what had happened. Lots of people wanted to talk to Abby. But she still felt sick from her cold. Her dad put his arm around her.

"Come on," he said. "We'll wait at Spencer's house until Mom comes home."

Mrs. Burton made them feel very comfortable. She got them blankets and made them soup. Rex curled up at Abby's feet. When Spencer got home from school, he let Abby hold Lily, too.

Spencer sat on the end of the couch and scratched Rex's head.

"Did he really save your life?" he asked.

Abby nodded. "He did. He's a hero."

"Yes, he is," Mrs. Burton agreed.

Abby turned to her dad. "I've been thinking. Maybe Rex doesn't have to stay out of my room. He can sleep there if he wants."

Mr. Larsen looked surprised. "Are you sure?" he asked.

Abby looked down at Rex's big, brown eyes. "I'm sure," she said with a smile.

One week later, Abby, Jia, and Spencer set up Rex's brand-new bed in her room. Abby's mom and dad had made it out of wood. It looked like a yellow castle with green vines painted on it. On the bottom was a big, comfy cushion for Rex to sleep on.

"That's the coolest bed ever," Spencer said.

"We should play princess," Jia said. "Rex's bed could be our castle. Rex can even be a friendly dragon."

"Or a king," Abby said. "The name

Rex means 'king,' you know."

Jia smiled. "Awesome!"

Then Abby noticed her princess calendar. "Oh, I almost forgot!" she said. "It's June first. I have to change the picture."

Abby looked at the month of May. Just few weeks ago, she did not have any pet at all. Now she had two pets. Two yellow pets. Two awesome pets! And one pet was even a hero.

Abby gave Rex a hug. "Rex, you are the best pet a princess could ever ask for!"

Make It Yourself!

Princess Photo Frame

Put a photo of your pet in this fun frame!

Level of Difficulty: Medium

(You'll need some help from a grown-up.)

You need:

- 6 large craft sticks
- yellow paint
- 3x5 or 4x6 photo
- 1 piece of cardboard, 5 ½" x 5 ½"
- glue
- scissors
- piece of yellow craft foam
- colored craft gems, fake flowers, and glitter paint pen
- small stick-on magnet

1. Paint the front of each craft stick yellow; let them dry.
2. Glue the photo on the center of your cardboard.
3. Glue one craft stick (yellow side up) to the left side of the cardboard, and another stick to the right side. Then glue two craft sticks to the top of the frame and two sticks to the bottom of the frame.
4. Cut the craft foam into the shape of a crown. Glue it to the top two craft sticks, centered above your picture.
5. Decorate the frame with gems, flowers, and pen. Don't forget to write your pet's name along the bottom.
6. Attach the stick-on magnet to the back so you can proudly display your pet's photo!

Royal Treat Holder

Turn a recycled container into a pretty place to store your pet's treats!

You need:

- empty round container with a lid (like an oatmeal container or coffee can)
- construction paper
- scissors
- pencil
- craft glue
- markers
- colored craft gems

1. Make sure your recycled container is clean and dry.
2. Remove the lid. Wrap construction paper around the container. If it's too long, draw a line with a pencil and then trim the paper to fit. If it's too short, overlap another piece of paper to cover the container.
3. Glue the paper to the container.
4. Decorate the container with the markers and gems. Then fill with your pet's favorite treats!

Don't forget: Both of these crafts have small parts—be sure to keep them out of reach of your pet!